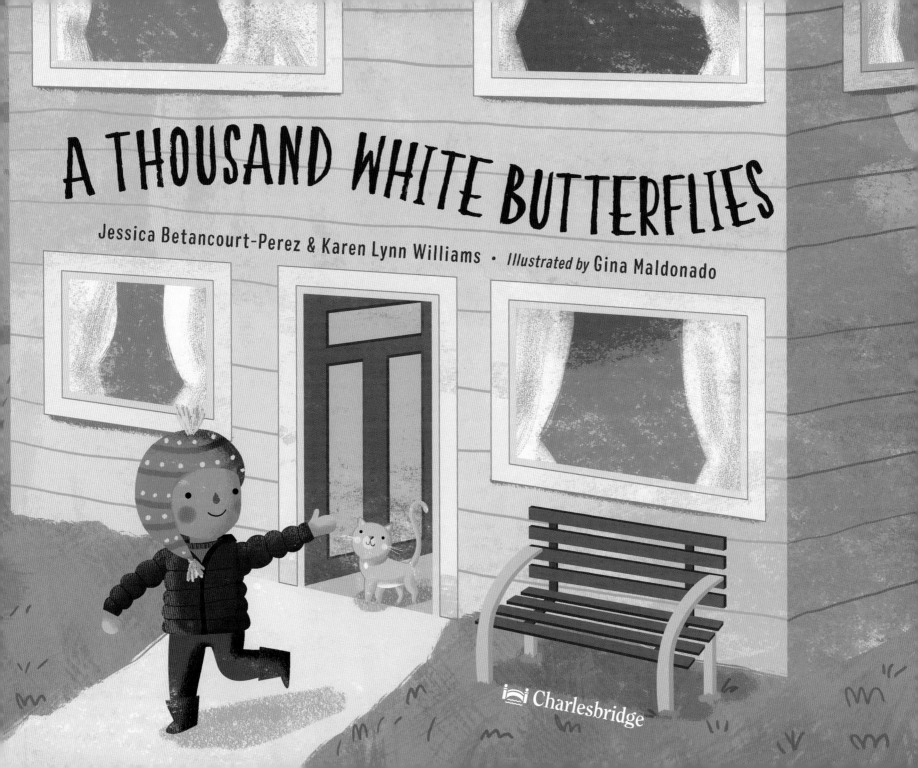

A THOUSAND WHITE BUTTERFLIES

Jessica Betancourt-Perez & Karen Lynn Williams • Illustrated by Gina Maldonado

Charlesbridge

THIS BOOK IS DEDICATED with love and affection to every immigrant who has had the courage to pursue their dreams in the United States and, like my grandmother, has led with example and shown other immigrants that it is possible to live a successful life in a foreign country—J. B. P.

IN LOVING MEMORY of my grandfather, who immigrated to the United States from Hungary at the age of sixteen—K. L. W.

PARA LOS NIÑOS de Latinoamérica que sueñan con un mejor futuro—G. L. M.

Text copyright © 2021 by Jessica Betancourt-Perez and Karen Lynn Williams
Illustrations copyright © 2021 by Gina Maldonado
All rights reserved, including the right of reproduction in whole or in part in any form. Charlesbridge and colophon are registered trademarks of Charlesbridge Publishing, Inc.

At the time of publication, all URLs printed in this book were accurate and active. Charlesbridge, the authors, and the illustrator are not responsible for the content or accessibility of any website.

Published by Charlesbridge
9 Galen Street, Watertown, MA 02472
(617) 926-0329 • www.charlesbridge.com

Illustrations created using textures made with crayons and acrylic paint, and colored digitally in Illustrator and Photoshop
Display type set in Shopwreck by Creativeqube
Text type set in Colby Condensed by Jason Vandenberg
Color separations by Colourscan Print Co Pte Ltd, Singapore
Printed by 1010 Printing International Limited in Huizhou, Guangdong, China
Production supervision by Brian G. Walker
Designed by Sarah Richards Taylor and Diane M. Earley

Library of Congress Cataloging-in-Publication Data
Names: Betancourt-Perez, Jessica, author. | Williams, Karen Lynn, author. | Maldonado, Gina Lorena, illustrator.
Title: A thousand white butterflies / Jessica Betancourt-Perez and Karen Lynn Williams; illustrated by Gina Maldonado.
Description: Watertown, MA: Charlesbridge, [2021] | Text primarily in English with Spanish words throughout. | Summary: Newly arrived from Colombia, Isabella's first day of school in the United States is cancelled because of snow and when Isabella notices a girl playing outside she makes a new friend, despite the language barrier.
Identifiers: LCCN 2019025355 (print) | LCCN 2019025356 (ebook) | ISBN 9781580895774 (hardcover) | ISBN 9781632898432 (ebook)
Subjects: LCSH: Immigrant children—Juvenile fiction. | First day of school—Juvenile fiction. | Snow—Juvenile fiction. | Friendship—Juvenile fiction. | CYAC: Snow—Fiction. | First day of school—Fiction. | Immigrants—Fiction. | Language and languages—Fiction. | Colombian Americans—Fiction. | Friendship—Fiction.
Classification: LCC PZ7.1.B479 Th 2021 (print) | LCC PZ7.1.B479 (ebook) | DDC [E]—dc23
LC record available at https://lccn.loc.gov/2019025355
LC ebook record available at https://lccn.loc.gov/2019025356

Printed in China
(hc) 10 9 8 7 6 5 4 3 2 1

OUTSIDE THE WINDOW, the United States is cold and gray.

The trees without leaves are lonely.

Like me.

I miss Papa, who is still in Colombia,
waiting for permission to travel.
My friends are there, too.

"Harás nuevos amigos en la escuela,"
Mama assures me.
I hope I will make new friends soon.

I wrap up in the soft ruana Papa gave me.
I count the days until the new year begins.

I get everything ready.
I have my brand-new jeans and
a fluffy orange sweater.

I packed my notebook and a little box with perfect crayons that I will share at school.

"¡Levántate!" Abuelita calls.
But I am already awake.

My first day of school in
the United States.
My make-new-friends day.
I will work hard to make
Papa proud.

"¡Mira!" Abuelita points out the window.
Everything is white, so white.
Mariposa wings dance in the sky.
It looks like a thousand white butterflies.

"Nieve," Abuelita says.
It's snow!

Mama turns on the TV.
We listen hard to the English.
School is canceled.

"Hay mucha nieve," Mama says.
I didn't know there could be too much snow.

Tears fall hot on my cheeks.
No new friends today.

I hate snow.
I think about Colombia,
warm and green.
There I had friends.

I drink milky, sweet taza de café.
And I draw a heart in the steam on
the window.
Te amo, Papa.

Oh! There is a girl outside.
She slips and slides on the sidewalk.

I sit up straight and watch.
She falls into the snow.
Buried.

Quick! I pull on my puffy jacket.

Stiff boots.

I feel like a statue in my mittens and hat.

I open the door. Whoosh!

Icy snow hits my face and slides down my neck.

"¿Estás bien?" I ask her.
The girl stands up, covered in snow.

She grins. "I made a snow angel.
You can make one, too."
I don't know all her words, but I
understand enough.

We both sink into the cold white powder
and wave our arms.

"I'm Katie." She points to herself.

"Soy Isabella." My voice is soft
like the snow.

"Let's build a snowman!" she exclaims.
I shrug and shake my head.
I don't know how.
"I'll show you," Katie says.

Katie tosses a snowball at me.

It bursts in my hands.

Round and round,

crunch, crunch, crunch.

We roll big balls of snow and pile them up.

Two stones for eyes, and one for the nose.
Abuelita gives us beads to make a mouth.
"¡Espera!" I run inside. Katie waits.

Katie helps me put Papa's ruana on the snowman.

We add a sombrero vueltiao.

We step back to look, and we both laugh.

Then it's time for her to leave.
"Tomorrow we will go to school together!"
Katie waves good-bye.
I wave back.

After dinner I draw a picture of me and Katie and our snowman with its smile the colors of Abuelita's beads.

I will send my drawing to Papa.

Outside my window the snow sparkles in the streetlights like silver-white butterfly wings.

It drapes the trees like a ruana.

The snow is soft and quiet, clean and new.
Beautiful.
When Papa calls, I will tell him,
"La nieve es hermosa."

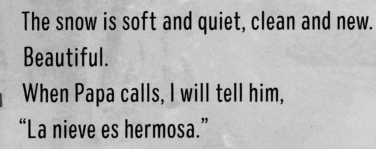

"Tengo una nueva amiga," I whisper in the dark.
Tomorrow I'll go to school. With my new friend.

AUTHORS' NOTES

I came to the United States from Colombia in 2005 when I was a teenager. My family split up in order to begin a new life in the United States with my grandmother, who was already here. We had to learn a new language and adapt to cultural differences in this new country. We were stronger than we could ever have imagined, and we overcame the many challenges. Happily, after seven years of hardship, my dad was able to reunite with us in the United States. We are a complete family again, and we are thankful for the opportunities that are offered in the United States. I am one of millions of immigrants who have journeyed to a new country for a better life.

—Jessica Betancourt-Perez

I met Jessica at a summer institute at Millersville University in Pennsylvania, where I was teaching. She wrote about coming to the United States from Colombia. Her brief paragraph told an important story with a simple arc, and I thought the story would be perfect for a picture book. It resonated with me in other ways, too. I am the granddaughter of immigrants to the United States, and I love snow. I went home after the institute and sat at my desk. I couldn't let go of this idea for a story. I contacted Jessica about coauthoring a picture book. Her enthusiasm for this project led to the joyful task of working together, learning, sharing, and creating.

—Karen Lynn Williams

MORE INFO

Immigrants are people who leave their original country to live permanently in a different country. Immigrants began coming to what is now the United States in the late 1400s. A large number of people arrived in the first part of the nineteenth century, and another wave came between the 1880s and the 1920s. Many Americans can trace their history back to immigrant relatives. People have come from all parts of the world to seek greater economic opportunity, religious freedom, and better lives for themselves and their families.

Immigrants and refugees from Colombia make up the largest group from South America in the United States today. They have fled violence, instability, persecution, and financial insecurity.

Like Isabella in the story, immigrants and refugees around the world are often separated from family members and friends. They must adjust to new climates and customs. They often miss their homeland, long for friendships, and look for a way to belong.

GLOSSARY

abuelita: "little grandmother" or "granny"; a loving diminutive of abuela

amigo/amiga: friend

Colombia: la República de Colombia; a country located at the northern tip of South America

en: in

es: is

escuela: school

espera: wait

¿Estas bien?: Are you OK?

hay: there is

harás: you will make

hermosa: beautiful

levántate: get up; a way to tell someone to wake up

mariposa: butterfly

mira: look

mucha: a lot

nieve: snow

nuevo/nueva: new

ruana: a warm garment from the Andes Mountain region of Colombia and Venezuela traditionally worn around both shoulders, sometimes sewn with an opening for the wearer to put their head through

sombrero vueltiao: a traditional Colombian hat

soy: I am

taza de café: a coffee drink, often served with lots of milk to children in Colombia

te amo: I love you

tengo: I have

un/una: one; a